Last Christmas
The Second Chances Lesbian Romance Series
by
Reba Bale

Table of Contents

Copyright

About This Book

Last Christmas they fell in love. This Christmas can they do it again?

Lucy

When I parked my tow truck behind a disabled vehicle that winter night, I had no idea that the love of my life was waiting for me inside. I took one look at Kate and fell head over heels in love. But then she betrayed me. Or so I thought...

Kate

Growing up in foster care, I learned to rely only on myself. Protecting my heart was a defense mechanism, until a sexy mechanic slipped right past my walls and made me believe in Christmas and fairy tales. But when Lucy dumped me, I realized that our love was all an illusion.

Now she's back, and after learning that she was wrong about what happened between us, she's pulling out all the stops to get us back together. But home cooked dinners, Christmas movies, and sweet gifts aren't enough to make me forget what happened last Christmas.

I made a mistake giving Lucy my heart once, and as much as I want the gift of love, I just don't know if I can trust her to stick around until New Year's Day, let alone forever.

Last Christmas is part of the *Second Chances Lesbian Romance* series. Each book in the series is a standalone sapphic romance featuring two strong women finding love the second time around.

Be sure to check out a free preview of Reba Bale's lesbian romance "The Divorcee's First Time" at the end of this book!

Dedication

To second chances, fresh starts, and remaining open to love.

Join My Newsletter

Want a free book? Join my weekly newsletter and you'll receive a fun subscriber gift. I promise I will only email you when there are new releases, free books, or special sales you'll want to see.

Visit my newsletter sign-up page at bit.ly/RebaBaleSapphic[1] to join today.

Lucy

"I hate this song!"

As soon as I heard Wham! singing the song about falling in love last Christmas, my fingers were stabbing at the buttons on my sister's car radio before I'd even slid fully into my seat.

"What? This used to be your favorite Christmas song," Denise reminded me.

That was true, until art imitated life. Like the singer, last Christmas I'd given someone my heart and they'd cruelly thrown it away. I didn't need to be reminded about it, especially at this time of the year. The wounds were still too fresh.

I gave her a meaningful look. "When I met Kate this song was playing on the radio. It was kind of our song."

My sister's face turned sympathetic. "I'm sorry. I didn't know that."

"How could you?"

Purposely shaking off my melancholy, I forced a smile. "Are you ready to get our shopping on?"

My sister and I went shopping the Monday after Thanksgiving every year. We waited for all the Black Friday shoppers to swoop in, then we picked up any remaining bargains while everyone else went back to work.

"I've got a purse full of credit cards and wish lists from all the sibs plus mom and dad," Denise responded. "I'm ready."

***

Last Christmas...

"I love this song!"

I shimmied my hips as I walked into the office, wiping my greasy hands on a cloth. The famous Wham! song played on the speakers in the lobby of DeNicola Automotive.

Being a mechanic was in my blood, and the garage was like a second home to me. I'd spent most of my life here, completely in love with cars since the day my father first handed me a wrench when I was three years old.

Of course, I just slammed it against the bumper, but I'd loved it, nonetheless.

"Lucy, you got a pick-up!"

My mother, who was also the office manager of DeNicola Automotive, held up a slip of paper. "Toyota Corolla on the side of Ogden Avenue near the mall. It's a roadside assistance referral. The lady thinks it's a radiator issue."

"Okay, I'll head out now."

Taking the slip of paper with the location of the stranded motorist, I headed out to the tow truck. It was just after four, so it was already getting dark, but the night was cool and clear. I inhaled deeply, smelling the faint scent of moisture in the air, and wondered if we'd finally get some snow. Illinois was having a late start to winter this year and we'd gotten all the way to December first without snow.

I spotted the car on the side of the road, hazard lights on, and pulled up behind the car. The old Corolla looked to be about twenty years old, although the body was in good condition. There was still steam rising from the hood of the car, confirming that the driver had a radiator issue.

When I walked up to the driver's side, I could see someone leaning back in the seat, their eyes fixed on their cell phone. I knocked the window and the woman inside jumped.

"DeNicola Automotive!" I shouted through the window.

The woman rolled down the window, and I could hear that same song about last Christmas that had been on in the office playing on the radio in the dashboard.

"Oh sorry! I was spacing out."

The woman's voice was soft and sweet. She looked to be in her early to mid-thirties, with brown hair that fell to her shoulders in soft waves, big brown eyes, and large, sensuous lips. My gaze fixed there longer than it should have and when she licked her lips, I couldn't help but groan internally as a wave of attraction practically knocked me over.

"Get a hold of yourself," I chastised myself mentally. "You're working, and you don't even know if she's single. Or gay."

Yet somehow as we stared into each other's eyes, I knew that my life was about to change, and this woman was going to be a part of it.

***

It turned out that Kate was in fact both gay and single. By the time I'd towed her car back to our garage, we were chatting like old friends. It seemed natural to walk up the street and have an early dinner while my father fixed her car.

Dinner stretched until the restaurant closed and by the next day, we were officially dating. From that point on, we were inseparable, spending all of our free time together.

I'd never believed in love at first sight before, until I met Kate. It was like I found the other half of my soul on the side of the road that day. We had six blissful months together, and I thought we'd live happily ever after.

Until we didn't.

Kate

"No, no, no! Not again!"

I slammed my fist against the steering wheel as my car made a clicking noise when I turned the key. The car was almost twenty years old, and it seemed ready to give up the ghost. Unfortunately, I didn't have money for a new car. Of course, I didn't have money for an expensive car repair either. When you lived paycheck to paycheck, there wasn't a lot of money left over for emergencies.

With a deep sigh, I pulled up the number for roadside assistance. As I talked to the dispatcher, I couldn't help but remember the last time I'd called for roadside assistance. It was almost this exact same time last year. My heart pinched as I remembered meeting Lucy, the only woman I'd ever loved.

When I'd rolled down the window and looked into a pair of large, dark brown eyes, I'd felt a jolt of emotion that was so strong it had taken my breath away. I hadn't been able to see much through a pair of shapeless overalls, but what I'd seen had been good.

Lucy was slim, with narrow hips and small breasts, just the right size to cup in my palms. Her hair was dark brown, almost black. And those eyes...I could stare in the chocolate brown depths for hours. And I had.

At least until she decided that I was cheating on her and broke up with me.

I sighed. I guess I should have fought more for Lucy, but I had been devastated by her accusations and the way she'd treated me. Besides, I wasn't one to grovel. After a lifetime of rejection, Lucy was just another person who didn't want me.

I thought I was over her by now, but with it being Christmas again, she kept popping into my mind at the most inconvenient moments. Like every time I heard that Wham! song on the radio or saw a commercial for a Christmas movie that we'd watched together.

Lucy and I had bonded over our shared love of food, comedies, dancing, and each other. The Christmas I'd spent with her had been the best holiday of my entire life.

Hearing a noise, I glanced up into the rearview mirror. The tow truck was here. I'd been a little nervous that it would be DeNicola Automotive but fortunately it was another company. I got out of my car and resolved to put Lucy out of my mind once and for all.

Fortunately, my car problem seemed to be a bad battery, so after getting a new one, I headed to the mall. I wanted to get going on my Christmas shopping and figured a Monday afternoon would be the perfect time, especially since I was off work today.

Most everyone else would be back at work after the long weekend I assumed, or too worn out by Black Friday shopping to come out again today.

I wandered through the stores, finding a few things for my friends and one of my foster mothers who I'd kept in touch with over the years. The mall was decked out for the holidays with Christmas decorations on every window, a giant sleigh with reindeer hanging on the ceiling, and in the very center of the mall, Santa himself. *Last Christmas* played on the speakers, just loud enough to hear over the noise of the mall. Despite my resolution to stop thinking about Lucy, she immediately popped into my mind.

***

Last Christmas...

"I love the mall at Christmas."

I gave Lucy a look even as I squeezed her hand. For most of my life, Christmas had just been another day, but Lucy's love of the holiday was contagious.

"Why do you love it?" I asked curiously.

"Everything is so festive with the lights and the decorations."

"And everyone is so cranky and stressed about the holiday," I said, nodding at a couple standing in front of a window, clearly arguing, while annoyed looking shoppers parted around them.

"My sibs and I used to love coming to see Santa," Lucy continued her reminiscing. "We'd look in the windows to find stuff to our lists for Santa, then we'd line up here and hand it to the big guy directly to make sure it didn't get lost in the mail or something."

Santa. That dude had repeatedly disappointed me when I was a kid. It's why as an adult I hadn't thought too much about the holiday. At least until lately...

There must have been something in my face that gave away my thoughts, because Lucy stopped, pulling me over to the side. She stepped close to me, and I could smell the mixture of citrus shampoo and motor oil that I'd always associate with her.

"What?"

"What?" I parroted the question back to her.

"You got a sad look just now."

I shook my head slightly. "It's nothing."

Lucy cupped my chin gently until I met her gaze. "It doesn't look like nothing."

"It turns out Santa can't find you when you're in foster care," I said with forced lightness. "That fat bastard doesn't have GPS on his sleigh I guess."

Lucy's face softened. "I'm sorry, I didn't realize..."

"It's fine, really," I said, pulling my chin away. "You couldn't know."

Of course Lucy couldn't know. She'd grown up in one of those families you see on television sitcoms and think don't exist. Except they did. I'd spent enough time with her and her family over the last few weeks to see just how loving and refreshingly normal they were. It was like visiting a foreign country.

Lucy pulled me into a tight hug.

"It's okay Kate, I know for a fact that Santa knows where my house is. I'll just let him know he can find you there from now on."

***

I watched the line of children waiting their turn to see the jolly old elf and felt another pang of sadness. Despite my upbringing, I'd always wanted to have kids. I imagined doing all the holiday things with them, like visiting Santa and picking out a tree and unwrapping a mountain of presents on Christmas morning.

But I wanted to do it as part of a couple. I was thirty-five now, maybe I should just give up on that idea and look into the best way to embrace life as a single mother. Not that I could afford to do that...

There was no sense in worrying about all this now, and I certainly shouldn't make any major life decisions on the spur of the moment. With a sad shake of my head, I turned around to head back towards the exit to the parking lot. I'd done enough shopping for the day.

Feeling a prickle on my neck, I looked up and saw Lucy coming towards me, a woman I recognized as her sister Denise by her side. My steps faltered. They were heading right towards me, there was no way I could pretend like I hadn't seen them.

Against my will I studied Lucy, noting any changes in her appearance. Her hair was a bit shorter now, but otherwise she looked almost exactly the same as she had the last time I saw her. The pain of losing her and the memory of her terrible accusations cut me like a knife.

I nodded in greeting, and Lucy gave me a glare. It figured. Like she had anything to glare at me about. I'm the one who should be glaring. I started to walk by her but stopped in shock when Lucy grabbed my wrist.

"Why?"

Her voice was filled with a pain that matched my own. I glanced towards her sister and then back to the face of the only woman I've ever loved. Her face was angry, but her eyes looked anguished.

"I'll ask you the same thing, Lucy, why? Why did you assume I was cheating? Why didn't you make the slightest effort to find out the truth? And why did you cut me out of your life as if I meant nothing?"

"I saw you hugging that woman on your front porch that morning," she reminded me. "You were only wearing a tee shirt!"

"Yeah, because I'd just woken up," I retorted. "To say goodbye to my cousin the flight attendant who'd surprised me with an overnight visit. And she was hugging me, not sticking her tongue down my throat."

It was the first time I'd even been able to give that much of an explanation. The last time I saw her, she'd refused to hear anything I said.

"Your cousin?" Lucy seemed confused.

"My cousin," I confirmed, pulling my hand away. "You threw everything we had away because of your jealousy and crappy assumptions. It could have all been cleared up with a conversation, but you couldn't even do me the courtesy of asking questions before you decided I'd betrayed you. And it's a damned shame too, Lucy, because I was in love with you. I thought you were the one."

I took off at a run, ignoring Lucy calling my name. Whatever she wanted to say, I didn't want to hear it. She' had already ripped my heart out once, there was no way I wanted to give her that power again.

Lucy

I stared after Kate in shock. Her cousin? Now that I thought back on what I saw six months ago, I could visualize that the other woman was wearing a navy blue uniform like a flight attendant might wear. And it's true, there was no kissing, just a short hug.

I'd woken up early that day and decided to surprise Kate with bagels for breakfast. Kate had literally never met a carb she didn't love. I'd pulled up in front of her house, seen her hugging someone on the porch, and without asking any questions, jumped to the assumption that she was cheating.

"Do you think she was telling the truth?" my sister asked. I had almost forgotten that she was here, I was so focused on seeing Kate.

I turned to face my sister, tears prickling my eyes. "I think she was. I remember her saying something about a cousin who dropped by sometimes when she had a flight into O'Hare. Oh my God, what have I done?"

When I saw Kate and the woman – her cousin? – on the porch that morning I drove away in a red hot rage. When Kate texted me to say 'good morning', I ignored her. I ignored multiple subsequent texts, hoping that she'd take a hint and go away.

Of course she didn't. She came to the garage when she got off work that day, wanting to check on me. And I, well I'd behaved horribly. I hadn't even let her get a word in edgewise as I screamed at her in front of everyone, calling her a cheater and a liar. All I had wanted was to hurt and humiliate her, the way she'd done to me.

Or so I thought.

If I'd been wrong about what happened, it changed everything. It meant I'd thrown away the only person who'd ever loved me besides my family. Thrown away the only woman I'd ever loved.

I clutched my sister's arm to keep myself from falling over with grief. "What am I going to do?"

She shook her head. "I don't know. We might have to bring in the rest of the siblings for this. You're going to need a grand gesture of epic proportions."

"Kate's not really a grand gesture person," I demurred. "I need to find another way. But I can fix this, right?"

My sister avoided my gaze. "I don't know, Lucy. For your sake, I hope so."

***

Last Christmas...

"That was...I don't even have words for whatever that was."

I looked up from where I was resting my head on Kate's shoulder. We were cuddled up in my bed, the air thick with the smell of sex. Or maybe that was just my imagination.

I was in shock. I'd known this woman for less than a week and she'd already become the most important person in my life. I'd fallen in love with her the minute I saw her and while we hadn't said the words yet – it was much too soon – we'd both been hinting around about it, so I knew that she felt the same.

It was like we were two parts of the same whole. Our lovemaking – and it had been lovemaking, not just sex – was explosive. We'd spent the better part of the last two hours exploring each other's bodies and wringing out orgasm after orgasm until we were both exhausted. And dehydrated.

I pushed to seated. "I need water. I'll be right back."

I moved quickly through my kitchen, grabbing items and heading back to the bedroom. Kate lay on top of the sheets, her arms bent behind her head, looking totally debauched.

I'd done that. And I planned to do it again after we rehydrated.

"Here's a water," I said, handing her a bottle. "And some chips."

She pushed herself up, leaning against the headboard to take a long swig of the water, completely comfortable with her nakedness. She was a little larger than me – taller, broader, and much curvier – but somehow, we fit together perfectly.

I joined her on the bed, taking a drink of my own water before resting my head against her shoulder.

"We're in a relationship now, right?"

Next to me, Kate chuckled. "My God, if every time we're together is like that, I won't be able to even look at someone else."

"So that's a yes?" I pressed.

She turned to meet my gaze. "I've never been one for relationships," she said softly. "But for you, I'm willing to try."

"Relationships are easy," I said. "You're each other's dates for weddings and events, you argue over the right way to hang the toilet paper, and you have lots and lots of sex. But only with each other."

"Toilet paper should be hung with the paper coming over the top of the roll," she said firmly.

"You're very wrong about that," I teased.

"No, I'm really not."

"See? Our first argument."

I moved until I was straddling her lap, then ran the water bottle across one nipple and then the other. She shivered as her nipples pebbled into hard points from the cold condensation on the outside of the bottle.

"There is one thing I know about relationships," she said, grabbing my bottle and setting it on the nightstand next to hers.

"What's that?" I asked.

"When you have a fight, you get to have make-up sex."

"Let's get to making up then."

Kate

I was in a funk the rest of the day, shaken to the core after running into Lucy at the mall. I supposed it was bound to happen eventually. We both lived in the same Chicago suburb, and it wasn't exactly huge. On some level I was surprised it hadn't happened already.

Unable to stand the thought of going home to an empty apartment, I headed over to the movie theater that was across the parking lot from the mall. As I waited in line, I debated between what I knew was a tearjerker love story, the latest superhero movie, a children's cartoon about toys, or a kidnapping movie. I decided that something mindless like a superhero movie would be just what I needed. I bought a ticket and a box of M&Ms, then hunkered down in my seat to watch the movie and take my mind off of what happened.

This close to winter solstice, it was already getting dark by the time I left the movies. I drove through Micky D's, dying for some greasy fries and a big old burger, then headed home. I frowned as I saw something on my porch. I hadn't ordered any packages.

Grabbing my bag of comfort food, I headed to the porch. As I got closer, I saw that the package was actually flowers, covered in paper to protect them from the cold temperatures.

That was weird, who would send me flowers?

Picking them up with my free hand, I headed into the house. I was too curious to wait to open the flowers, putting them on the countertop and carefully removing the paper that protected them. Inside was a giant vase full of yellow daisies. I knew who sent them before I even read the card.

***

Last Christmas...

"When we get married, what kind of flowers will you carry?"

I frowned as I looked up from between Lucy's legs. We'd spent the night together and I woke up hungry for the taste of her.

"You're asking me questions about flowers while I'm licking your pussy?" I asked incredulously. "I must not be doing this right."

When I made to pull away, she laughed and tightened her thighs around my shoulders, holding me in place. I flattened my tongue, running it from the bottom of her channel to the top. When I touched her clitoris, Lucy punched her hips up and moaned.

"Still thinking of something else?" I teased as I pulled away.

Lucy pinned me with an intense look.

"A girl can daydream about happily ever after, can't she? Especially when you make me feel like this. It's never been like this with anyone else."

I stifled the intense longing I felt. I wanted to daydream too. But we'd been together for only a couple of weeks. It was too soon to dream about forever, right?

"C'mon, what flowers would you pick?" she asked. "I'd pick lilies."

I met her eyes for a long moment. "Daisies," I said. "A whole big bouquet of yellow daisies. Now be quiet so I can have my breakfast."

She sighed my name as my tongue slid between her folds again.

***

I stared at the bouquet. It had to be from her, right? With a deep sigh, I plucked the little envelope out of the flowers, slicing it open with the edge of one fingernail.

Kate, I was wrong. So very wrong. I'm so sorry about everything. XOXO Lucy

My eyes fixated on the XOXO, wondering what it meant. Then a righteous anger filled my body. She was sorry? She'd made me trust her and then ripped my heart right out of my chest. And she thought flowers would make up for it?

I crumpled up the note and threw it in the trash, and started to do the same for the daisies, but stopped at the last minute. There was no sense wasting good flowers. Instead, I put them in the middle of my kitchen table, grudgingly admitting that they really brightened up the tiny space.

As I ate my Micky D's, I tried to put Lucy out of my mind. But it proved harder than I thought it would. I tossed and turned all night, thinking about her and everything that had happened.

Somehow, I wasn't surprised when she texted me the next morning. Lucy was nothing if not persistent. It was one of the things I loved about her. Used to love, I mean.

Did you get the flowers? Can we get together so I can apologize in person?

I ignored her message, and another one came two hours later. I blocked her number without reading it. Whatever she wanted to say, I didn't want to hear it.

Lucy

I sighed deeply as I checked my phone for about the hundredth and seventeenth time today. Two days had passed since I ran into Kate at the mall. I'd sent flowers twice, sent cookies, texted multiple times, and finally called her directly, hoping she would pick up. That's when I realized that she had blocked my number.

"Maybe you should let it go," my sister Denise said. "She obviously doesn't want to talk to you."

"I have to keep trying," I said stubbornly. "I never got over her."

"I know, but sometimes things just aren't meant to be."

"What are you girls talking about?" my mother said, walking out to the back porch where Denise and I were talking. "You look very serious."

"We saw Kate at the mall the other day," I told her.

"Did you punch her?" Mom asked loyally.

I shook my head miserably. "She told me what happened that day. The woman was her cousin, a flight attendant who'd surprised her with an overnight visit. She said she never cheated on me."

"And do you believe her?" Mom asked, studying me carefully.

"As soon as she told me what happened, I remembered her telling me about a close cousin who came to town every now and again. I jumped to the wrong conclusion."

"Well, why didn't she tell you then?" Mom asked. "If there was nothing to hide it seems like she would have spoken up."

"I never gave her a chance," I said miserably. "First, I ghosted her, and then when she came to see me, I called her a cheater and a liar. Honestly, I never even considered that there was another explanation besides her cheating on me, so I shut her down without even talking about it."

Mom leaned against the porch rail, giving me a stern look.

"So, you've been miserable this entire year because of your own doing?"

"Yeah." I sighed deeply.

"You know, I always thought it was weird that Kate would cheat on you. That girl looked at you like you hung the moon and the stars. You seemed perfect for each other."

"We *are* perfect for each other."

"Do you still love her?" Mom asked.

"I never stopped loving her."

"Sounds like you've got some groveling to do then."

I sighed again. "I'm trying."

***

Last Christmas...

"What are you doing?"

Kate glanced up, squinting against the light in the hallway beaming through the open door. She'd been sleeping beside me but when I woke up, she was gone. She was wrapped up in a blanket, sitting in the window seat in my living room, staring out at the softly falling snow.

"I couldn't sleep," she responded.

"Maybe you need my grandmother's special sleepy time drink."

"Sleepy time drink?" she asked.

"Yeah, it's a secret family recipe. You stay here and I'll make you one."

I clicked on the lights of the Christmas tree and then headed into the kitchen. After finding all the ingredients, I mixed up my Grandma's recipe, then brought out two steaming mugs of Sleepy Time Drink in my hands. I placed the mugs on the small table next to the window seat, then tapped her legs.

"Scoot over."

She hugged her knees up to her chest, and I sat across from her, sliding my legs under the blanket. When she stretched her legs back out, I tangled mine with hers.

"Try it," I told her, nodding toward the two mugs.

I grabbed one, handing it to her, and then I grabbed the second one, bringing it up to my face. It smelled like chocolate and cinnamon and memories. Kate took a sip, then coughed.

"Holy shit! Does the secret family recipe include a shit-ton of whiskey?"

She smiled, her face so sweet and beautiful in the moonlight that it made my breath catch.

"I'll never tell."

I took another sip, enjoying the play of the sweet chocolate with the other ingredients.

"How come you couldn't sleep?" I asked.

She shrugged. "Sometimes I get insomnia. It's been happening since I was a kid."

"Probably because your grandma never made you a Sleepy Time Drink."

"Yeah, I never knew my grandmother."

I bit my lip to keep from apologizing. Sometimes I forgot that Kate grew up in a very different environment than I did. As far as she knew, she had no family anywhere, and she didn't remember her parents. But she also hated it when people felt sorry for her about her rough upbringing.

"Did your mom make this for you too?" she asked curiously.

"My mom is more of a chamomile tea person. It's my dad's mother who enjoys booze." I laughed to myself, thinking of the differences between my mom and her fiery Italian mother-in-law. "Those two are like night and day, but you'll see that at Christmas dinner."

She stilled. "Christmas dinner?"

I gave her a rueful look. "Oh yeah, would you like to join me and my family for Christmas? I already told my mother I was going to bring you."

"I wouldn't want to impose."

Kate had the cutest habit of taking everything very seriously, never wanting to be 'a bother'.

"There will be liked a hundred of us there, they'll never even notice you."

"A hundred?" she laughed.

"Well, not quite a hundred, but all my sibs will be there, some of whom have kids and significant others, and my parents and both sets of grandparents. So it'll be a full house for sure—loud, crazy, and with tons of good food. You'll definitely want to wear something with a stretchy waistband."

"Oh well, that's sweet of you, but..."

I interrupted her. "My entire family is dying to meet the woman who's stolen my heart."

I took another sip of my drink while she considered my words. The whiskey warmed my body from the inside out.

"I'm not too experienced with family stuff," she said softly.

Although Kate had had serious girlfriends over the years, they'd never gotten to the 'meet the family' stage. I wondered if she'd kept herself apart from family holidays on purpose, uncomfortable with participating in rituals she wasn't familiar with.

I rubbed my legs against hers and met her gaze so she could see the truth in my words.

"Don't worry, my family is going to love you, just like I do."

Kate

I couldn't say I was surprised when I came home from work and found Lucy sitting on the steps of my apartment. I lived in a triplex on the north side of town, only a short ride from most of the stores and businesses. It wasn't anything fancy, but it was what I could afford with my job as a hotel hospitality manager. Hospitality manager was just a fancy way of saying that I was the supervisor of all the hotels maids and janitorial staff. It was hard work, but it was a living.

Growing up in foster care, I wasn't able to go to college like some of my friends. I'd thought a lot about going now, maybe getting a degree in business or even something totally different, but I hadn't gotten around to enrolling yet. Or I was too scared to make a change after all this time.

***

Last Christmas...

"How was your day?"

Lucy looked adorable as she smiled at me over the island that separated her kitchen from the living room. She was wearing an apron over her clothes, and she had a smudge of flour on her cheek, likely from the homemade pasta she'd promised me. I could smell her grandmother's marinara sauce simmering on the stove.

I'd never dated a foodie before, and I found I really liked it.

"It was okay," I said. "We had a lot of asshole customers, so I kept having to help diffuse things."

She gave me a sympathetic smile and nodded towards the counter. "I already opened some wine. Help yourself."

Almost as comfortable in her home as my own after a few weeks of dating, I went to the cabinet to grab some glasses, pouring us both a glass of the red wine that Lucy said went best with pasta. I liked wine, but I knew nothing about it. Lucy, however, was a wine connoisseur, which struck me as funny given her career as a mechanic.

That was Lucy though, she was the most fascinating mix of contradictions.

She served us up huge plates of pasta, then we sat across the table from each other.

"Can I ask you something?"

"Yeah," I responded.

"It doesn't seem like you like your job too much."

"It pays the bills," I shrugged. "When you don't have a college degree and you haven't gone to trade school, it's hard to get anything that's not service work."

"What if you got one?" she asked.

"One what?" I knew what she was saying but I was stalling, the tiniest bit uncomfortable with where this conversation was going.

"A college degree. You could start taking classes at community college, then transfer for your last two years. I know a lot of classes are online now so you can take them around your work schedule."

I twirled my spaghetti around my fork, not looking at her.

"I don't know if I'm cut out for college."

"Why not? You're one of the smartest people I know," she said firmly.

Her praise made my heart feel funny. I'd never really had someone on my side like this before.

"I guess I could probably take some business classes," I said finally. "It would help me in my job, maybe make me more likely to get promoted to another department."

Lucy chewed thoughtfully. "Let me ask you another question. If you could do anything you wanted – any career, with money as no object – what would you do?"

"I'd be a social worker," I answered immediately, surprising myself. "I'd help kids like me who were in foster care."

"That's what you should do then," she said. "Start taking social work classes at community college and if you like it, you can get your degree and stop working for peanuts at the hotel."

"Well, I don't think social workers make a lot of money either," I told her.

"It wouldn't matter if you were in a job you love. You deserve to do something that makes you happy."

***

"What are you doing here, Lucy?" I asked.

She pushed to her feet with a small smile of greeting. She looked nervous.

"I was hoping we could talk."

"The time for talking would have been six months ago," I reminded her. "Before you dumped me."

She winced. "Yeah. I know. And I know you don't owe me anything but please, can we just talk for a few minutes?"

"Fine," I grumbled. "But I haven't eaten all day so make it fast."

We had three maids out with COVID, so I'd had to help make up rooms and clean the lobby. It was hard work, and I was exhausted.

"How about dinner?" she said quickly. "We could go to that diner up the street."

We'd spent a lot of time there when we were dating, popping in for breakfast after a long night of lovemaking, or stopping for a late night dinner after we were out dancing. As much as I liked the food there, I hadn't been there once since we broke up.

"Fine, but you're buying."

Lucy

I watched Kate across the table as she fiddled with her napkin, trying to remember the speech I'd planned for exactly this moment. Unfortunately, my mind was a complete blank. All I could do was stare at Kate and think about how much I loved her and how I'd do anything to get her back now that I knew the truth.

She looked a little thinner than she'd been when we dated, and her hair was a little bit longer. Dark circles shadowed her eyes. It made me worried about her.

The waitress came and took our orders – a BLT with fries for Kate and a Cobb salad for me – then Kate pinned me with a serious look.

"Well?"

"I don't know if I ever told you this, but my very first girlfriend cheated on me. It was in college, and we'd gone to the same party together. I lost track of Sonia and when I found her, she was sitting on another woman's lap, kissing her and grinding on her."

Kate's expression didn't change but she did ask a question. "You went to college?"

I was surprised it had never come up before, but then again, I knew that Kate was self-conscious about not having a degree, so I likely never mentioned it. The speakers over my head started playing an instrumental version of the last Christmas song, and I took it as a sign.

"Yeah. I always knew I wanted to work in the garage, but my mother was adamant that I go to college and 'explore my options' for careers." I made air quotes and imitated my mother's nasally voice. "So, I went to U of I and got a degree in business. Then I came right back to the garage where I could do what I love."

It was true too. I loved nothing more than working on engines, puzzling out how to make them work better, rebuilding them and restoring them to their past glory. I loved the smell of engine grease more than anything else – except maybe Kate.

In addition to working as a mechanic, I was learning the administrative side of the business too. My father had already promised that my brother and I could buy him out of the garage when he retired.

"Anyway, the situation with Sonia messed with my head. I thought we were in love. I mean, I was in love, she just wasn't. And somehow, all these years later, I realized it was still in the back of my mind, the idea that I could be in love with someone and think everything was going great, but they'd be cheating on me. When I saw you with your cousin, I thought...well, you know what happened."

"I thought you knew me better than that," she choked, like she was trying not to cry. "I thought I knew you better than that too. The way you treated me when I came to talk to you..."

"I know Kate, and I'm so damned sorry that I didn't trust you enough to give you a chance to explain who the woman was." My voice was thick with regret.

"If you'd just gotten out of the damned car instead of racing off in a fury you would have met my cousin and knew right away that the story you'd created in your head was wrong. But you didn't. Instead, you chose to ghost me, and then humiliate me in front of your family and your customers. There's no coming back from that, Lucy."

We both paused as the waitress dropped off our food. I looked around, taking in the tinsel and holly that decorated the walls and counter. Through the window, I could see the Greek man who owned the place racing around the kitchen. Once the waitress had left the table, I turned back to Kate.

"I need you to know, when I saw you in the mall, I realized that I love you. I still love you I mean. I never stopped."

"And how do you expect me to respond to that, Lucy?" Her tone was angry. "Am I supposed to forget what happened and just go back to how things were last Christmas?"

She took a bite of her sandwich that was almost violent, chewing so hard I was surprised she didn't crack her tooth.

"Can we just start over?" I asked.

"Why would we do that when things went so badly last time?" She took another angry bite of her sandwich.

"Because I love you. And because I think you still love me. We were good together Kate. I just...I don't want to let this misunderstanding keep us from a lifetime of happiness together."

"Misunderstanding?" she said sarcastically. "Is that what we're calling it now?"

I winced, even though I knew I deserved her ire. I leaned forward, waiting until she met my eyes.

"I fucked up. Majorly fucked up. I would give anything to go back in time and punch myself in the face, do something, anything, to keep from hurting you, but I can't."

I took a deep breath.

"All I'm asking is that you give me a second chance Kate. Give me a chance to prove that I learned from my mistake, that I've grown as a person, and that I'll never, ever treat you like that again."

She dropped her sandwich and leaned back against the cracked vinyl booth.

"I would have to be crazy to give you another chance after how you treated me."

I could tell she was wavering, so I gave her a half smile.

"Well, you always were a little crazy," I teased, desperate to lighten the mood.

She sighed deeply.

"Fine, we can talk. Maybe go on a date. And if that works out okay, we can go on another. But I swear to God Lucy, if you ever treat me like that again, you will *not* get a third chance. Please, don't make me sorry that I agreed to this."

My smile widened and I reached across the table, squeezing her hand in mine. Just like I remembered, little currents of electricity seemed to hum right where our skin touched. I wondered if it would always be like this. Because now that Kate was giving me a second chance, I wasn't backing down until I had my ring on her finger.

***

Last Christmas...

"How do you feel about marriage?"

Kate choked a little on her baked potato. "Marriage?"

She said it like I was speaking in a foreign language.

"Yeah, you know, two people standing in front of their friends and family, pledging their love, then eating cake and drinking champagne."

"You're describing a wedding, not marriage," she teased.

She had the cutest smile. One side of her mouth quirked up higher than the other and her eyes sparkled with amusement.

"I was just thinking that maybe someday, if things go well, we might be the ones getting married."

Kate set her fork down, leaning forward in her chair. I leaned forward in response.

"Did anyone ever tell you that you're not supposed to talk about getting married on the first date?" she asked incredulously.

"Can we talk about it on the second date then?"

"There's going to be a second date?" she asked, her tone bemused.

"Of course. This has been the best date ever, we definitely need to do it again."

She shook her head at me like I was crazy. "Are you free tomorrow?"

Kate

I was probably an idiot. No, scratch that, I was definitely an idiot. It wasn't like me to forgive something so egregious as what Lucy had done and yet, I couldn't help but give in.

The truth was I was still in love with Lucy. All it had taken was one look at her when we met at the mall for me to know that our months of absence – and her terrible betrayal – had done nothing to cool my ardor. Even sitting here eating a sandwich my nipples were hardening against my bra, desperate to feel her fingers on them again.

But I meant what I said. Lucy had to earn my trust. The first time around, we rushed into a physical relationship the day after we met, then fell into a girlfriend/girlfriend relationship. It was hot and heavy and clearly way too fast.

If we were going to do this again, we needed to take our time. Get to know each other better. Set boundaries. Work on communication.

It was a lot to take in, but I felt cautiously optimistic.

Now that we'd agreed to try again, by unspoken agreement we shifted into small talk, chatting about the things that had happened in our lives since we broke up. Lucy told me about her niece who'd been born three months ago, and the new car she was restoring in her off-hours in her father's home garage. I told her about the way the roof to my apartment caved in during that big storm last spring, and how it meant that my cheap ass landlord finally had to replace the disgusting carpets in my living room.

It was funny the way we fell right back into easy conversation, as if no time had passed.

***

Last Christmas...

"Holy crap, it's almost midnight." Lucy looked around the sports bar where we'd met up for dinner nearly six hours ago. "It's so weird. Usually, I hate small talk but for some reason with you, I feel like I could talk forever."

I knew exactly what she meant. The time had flown by while we were talking, the exact same way that it had happened on our first two dates, and yet I felt like I could talk to her for another six hours. It was our third date in three days, and already I felt like I'd known Lucy forever.

We settled the bill, then walked to the parking lot, laughing when we realized that somehow, we'd parked our cars side by side. It had started snowing while we were inside, leaving a thin layer of snow on our cars. The parking lot was quiet and the lights reflecting on the snow made it seem like the ground was glowing.

"It's a sign," Lucy said.

"A sign of what?" I asked.

"A sign that we're meant to be. We're each other's soul mate."

The minute the words were out of her mouth she clasped her hand over it.

"Oh my God, I'm sorry, it's probably too soon for talk like that."

I stepped closer, backing her up against the side of her car. "It's not too soon if it's true."

I put my hands on the roof of her car, on either side of her head, and shifted until only inches separated us.

"What are you doing?" she asked breathlessly.

I could tell by the twinkle in her eye she knew exactly what I was doing. "I'm going to kiss you now."

I closed the distance between our lips, pressing against the softness of hers, and I was immediately excited. I licked along the seam of her lips, then slid my tongue inside her mouth, exploring hers. I could taste the beer and hot wings that we'd shared on her breath.

Lucy wrapped her arms around my waist, pulling me even closer. I tilted my head, deepening the kiss, and every cell in my body seemed to be singing with joy. This was it. I'd finally found The One. The kind of love I'd secretly *been dreaming about ever since I was a little girl, even before I knew that I was queer.*

When we pulled apart, we were both breathing heavily. I rested my forehead against hers, staring into her eyes.

"That might have been the most perfect first kiss I've ever had," I whispered.

"I think we can do better," Lucy said, her eyes sparkling.

"Do you now?"

"Oh yeah, but you're gonna have to come home with me to find out."

"Are you asking me to spend the night with you?" I teased.

"Baby, I'm asking you to spend forever with me."

***

"How is this going to work?" Lucy asked as we exited the café.

"Well, I guess I'll unblock your number, and you can text me or something."

"How about dinner Friday night?" she suggested. "You can come to my place, and I'll make you your favorite pasta."

"I'm not just going to fall back into a relationship with you Lucy," I said firmly. "That's what got us in trouble in the first place."

"No, my trust issues are what got us in trouble," she corrected. "But I promise, when you come over for dinner, we will not have sex."

I felt my pussy clench in disappointment. She was all on board with resuming all of our previous activities right now. I ignored that greedy bitch.

"This time, we'll take it slow," Lucy promised.

"Well, maybe not that slow," I thought to myself, given that I was already picturing us together again. I hadn't had sex since we broke up – at least not with another person – and I was dying to get my hands on Lucy's svelte little body again.

Out loud I said, "Let's just play it by ear."

Lucy

I walked Kate back to her house, our shoulders and fingers occasionally brushing each other as we walked side by side on the narrow sidewalk. The air was crisp and cool, hinting of snow soon.

"Can I give you a hug?" I asked as we reached Kate's house.

"Okay."

I pulled her into my arms slowly, gently. She stood stiffly in my embrace then softened in stages until her head was resting on my shoulder. I called that a win. This close I could smell the citrus fragrance of her shampoo. I smelled her hair like a weirdo and held her tight.

"Can I call you tomorrow?" I whispered. "I can call you after work and we can get started on getting to know each other again."

"Yeah." She pulled away, giving me a long searching look before turning and heading into her apartment without another word.

I headed towards my car, cautiously optimistic.

Kate and I texted several times over the next few days, both of us clearly trying not to just pick up where we left off but to start fresh. It felt like the right approach for both of us. Our initial texts were a bit stilted, but we warmed up as we went along, enough that I was feeling positive about Kate agreeing to come over for dinner on Friday.

I changed my outfit like five times, debating between super casual and sexy. I finally settled on a faded pair of jeans and a baby blue V-neck sweater that hugged my curves without being too over the top sexy.

When Kate knocked on the door Friday night, I had marinara sauce simmering on the stove and a big salad ready to go. I just needed to cook the pasta and cut the loaf of garlic bread and we'd be good to go.

"Hey, thanks for coming," I greeted her with a smile.

Kate looked like maybe she wasn't certain about staying. She stood on the porch with all her muscles tightened, like she was ready to flee. Not that I could blame her for that.

***

Six months ago...

"Lucy, Kate is here for you."

My mother stuck her head in the garage, her eyes concerned. Probably because last night I'd spent hours on her couch crying my eyes out to her, telling her about Kate's betrayal. She'd encouraged me to talk to Kate, but instead I'd deleted all of her texts and voicemails and leaned into my misery.

Wiping my hand on a rag, I stalked out to the lobby. Kate rushed toward me as soon as I cleared the door, a look of concern on her face.

"Lucy! Are you okay? I was worried when I hadn't heard from you for three days."

We'd been texting and chatting multiple times a day since the day I picked her up with my tow truck. I'd ignored all of her efforts at contact since the day I saw her on the porch with her other lover.

"You have a lot of nerve coming here!" I exploded.

Out of the corner of my eye, I could see my father and brother walking in from the garage area. In the waiting area, two customers watched with avid interest.

"What do you mean? Are you mad at me or something? Is that why you've been ghosting me?"

"Did you think you could hide it?" I answered her question with a question of my own.

"Hide what?" She looked confused.

"That you're cheating on me!"

In the waiting room, one of the customers gasped.

All the blood left Kate's face.

"What are you talking about? I'm not cheating on you. I would never do that."

She reached out a hand towards me, then dropped it. "Lucy, where is this coming from?"

Enraged by what I thought was her further deceiving me, I lashed out. Voice raised, hands waving, I called her a liar. A cheat. A low-class slut. Through it all, she stood stoically, her face a blank slate. I told myself that her expression was proof that she was a cheater. After all, she wasn't even denying it or trying to argue. I completely ignored the look of hurt and betrayal in her eyes.

When I finally wound down, Kate shook her head sadly.

"I knew this was too good to be true."

Then she turned on her heel and walked out of the garage and out of my life. I slid to the floor and started crying.

***

"Come on in." I motioned with my hand. "Dinner's almost ready."

Kate stepped inside and took off her coat, placing it on the rack by the door, and then followed me into the kitchen.

"Smells good."

Despite my tomboy upbringing, my mother had insisted that I learn how to cook. I was glad for that, not only because it came in handy, but also because I actually enjoyed it.

"Do you need help?"

"How about you open a bottle of wine while I finish up here?" I suggested. "Then you can set the table if you don't mind."

"Sure."

We worked together in silence, each of us lost in our own thoughts. Once Kate set the table, I brought out the food, and we settled into our seats. The scene was so familiar it made my heart pinch. I held up my glass of wine.

"To second chances and fresh starts."

Kate looked at me for a long moment before lifting her glass to mine. I released a breath as she parroted, "To second chances and fresh starts."

Kate

I stared across the table at Lucy, my mind swirling. This felt like dozens of nights we'd spent together, and yet it was different. Now I knew how Lucy could turn on me, how easy it was for her to cut me out of her life. Now I knew about the pain of losing someone you love.

With my background, I didn't trust easily. I think that's what had bothered me most that day I'd gone to the garage and been publicly shamed by Lucy. As she yelled at me, insulted me, and accused me of something I hadn't done, I remember thinking that I couldn't believe I'd let my guard down for her. I couldn't believe I'd trusted her, and envisioned a happily ever after for us.

For weeks I'd chastised myself for being a sucker, for letting her slip past my defenses, and for letting myself get carried away in the fairy tale of love at first sight. I promised myself that I'd never make a mistake like that again.

And yet, here I was in Lucy's house, toasting to fresh starts. Her apology had seemed sincere, and the fact was, she was right. I was still in love with her. She claimed to love me too. I'd seen the devastation on her face when I'd finally been able to explain who the woman on my porch was. I didn't think she'd faked that.

Then again, we should have had that conversation six months ago. Instead of just assuming I was some kind of cheating slut, Lucy should have talked to me. One of the things I'd loved about our time together was the way we could talk forever. At least I thought we could. But maybe we just hadn't talked about anything important.

Lucy hadn't just been my girlfriend, in our short time together she'd also become my best friend. I'd lost both when she dumped me. And six months later, I still hadn't recovered. That's really why I was here.

"You look like you're thinking awful hard over there," Lucy said lightly. Her eyes studied me carefully though.

"I was wondering how we got so serious so fast before, when we clearly didn't know each other very well."

"We knew each other in all the ways that mattered," Lucy countered.

"I disagree. You didn't know me well enough to realize I would never cheat on someone," I said. "And I didn't know you well enough to know that you'd publicly humiliate me instead of talking to me about your fears. After all the talking we did, the one time we needed to talk most, you shut me out."

Lucy's eyes filled with tears, but she blinked them away. I wasn't trying to hurt her. I wanted to understand what happened. If we were doing a fresh start, how could I know it wouldn't happen again?

***

Last Christmas...

"Who's this?"

Lucy glanced at the Christmas tree ornament I was holding. It was a green wreath with a picture in the center. Lucy was pressing her lips against another woman's cheek while the woman smiled for the camera. They looked young and happy. The woman was kind of fancy, wearing a lot of make-up and expensive-looking earrings. Definitely not the type of woman I would expect Lucy to be with.

"Oh. That's Sonia. I dated her for a year in college." A shadow passed Lucy's eyes as she studied the picture. "I didn't even know I still had that."

"Bad breakup?" I guessed.

She nodded. "Yeah, it was really terrible. I thought we'd be together forever, but it wasn't meant to be."

Her face flashed with remembered pain, making me want to hurt whoever this Sonia was, the same way she'd hurt Lucy. I dropped the ornament back into the box, not wanting to see it anymore, but Lucy plucked it out and marched it to the trash can, dropping it on top of the takeout containers from dinner.

"Have you seen her since you broke up?" I asked curiously.

"Oh yeah, we had a lot of classes together and several mutual friends, so I saw her pretty frequently for my last year of college at U of I."

"That must have sucked." I hadn't had any serious long-term relationships, but I knew how awkward it could be to run into an ex.

"The crazy thing was, after we'd been broken up for a while, right when I was getting over her, she had the nerve to ask me to get back together with her."

"Did you get back together?" I asked curiously.

"No way. I never go back for seconds."

***

"Do you remember when we were decorating your tree last year and I found that ornament with a picture of you and your ex?" I asked.

Lucy chewed a spoonful of pasta before answering. "Yeah, vaguely."

"You told me that the two of you had a bad breakup, and then later she tried to get back together with you."

"That's right. Why do you ask?"

"I remember you saying something like, 'I don't go back for seconds' as a reason that you didn't want to get back together with her."

She gave me a thoughtful look.

"Yeah, that sounds like something I would say. I probably didn't want to go into all the details with you about how she was a lying, cheating bitch."

I flinched a little, remembering how she'd called *me* a lying, cheating bitch only six months ago. Lucy saw it in my face, and dropped her fork so she could reach for my hand. I felt a hum of electricity where our skin touched, the same as always. Even after everything that had happened, my body still wanted her. I still wanted her.

"You're not like her," she said softly. "I understand that now. I promise I'll never fly off the handle like that again, Kate. I was having a trauma response, and I wasn't thinking clearly. It's not an excuse, but it is an explanation of why I reacted the way I did. I'll do anything – anything – to make it up to you and prove that I'm worthy of you."

I sighed softly. I wanted so much to believe her, but I'd need some time.

"Let's just eat and go from there," I suggested, taking a bite of my pasta. "This is delicious, by the way."

It was, too. One of the things that I'd missed about dating Lucy was all of the incredible homemade pastas and special sauces. I'd gained five pounds during the time we were dating.

We finished dinner, both of us relaxing more as the night went on. It was like old times, sharing a meal, chatting, laughing. After we finished, I helped Lucy clean up, moving around each other as she washed the pots and I loaded the dishwasher.

"What should we do now?" I asked as I dropped a cleansing tablet in the dishwasher and closed the door.

When I turned around, Lucy was right behind me, close enough that when I took a deep breath, our bodies almost touched. The air between us seemed to heat up.

Slowly, giving me ample time to push her away, Lucy lifted her hand to cup my cheek. Our eyes met, and we stared at each other for what seemed like hours before she swayed towards me. I met her halfway.

Lucy

I'd told myself I wouldn't try anything with Kate tonight. I knew she needed time, we both needed time, to heal from what happened. But seeing her here in my kitchen, working together like we'd done so many times, I just couldn't resist getting closer.

If she'd pushed me away, stepped back, given me any indication that she wanted me to move away from her, I would have done it in an instant. But instead she stared into my eyes, her gaze full of longing. When I dropped my eyes, I saw her pulse pounding furiously in her neck.

Deciding to follow my instincts, I pressed my lips against hers. Our lips met for maybe five seconds before the attraction that was always simmering below the surface exploded. Our bodies smashed together, lips and teeth fighting for control.

Kate dug her fingers into my hair, tugging at the strands until I felt the sting in my scalp. I lowered my hands to cup the delicious curves of her ass. I couldn't get enough of her, kissing her with a desperation that would have scared me if I'd been thinking clearly.

I backed her up to the counter and lifted her so I could press my way between her thighs. She groaned against my lips but didn't protest. Instead, she tightened her thighs around my hips, pulling me even closer as the kiss went on and on.

Kate's hands slid down from my head, tracing over my shoulders and chest before frantically unbuttoning my shirt. I groaned as she cupped my breasts through my bra, her touch firm and commanding. My nipples hardened against her palms.

I wanted to take her here. I wanted nothing more than to lay her out on the counter, bare that beautiful pink pussy, and tease her until she released her cream all over my tongue. But it was too soon. I'd promised her that we wouldn't have sex tonight. We needed to keep tonight's activities PG. Or at least PG-13.

I was playing the long game here. Delaying our satisfaction now would hopefully set us up for longer term success this time around. Regretfully, I pulled back just enough to break the kiss before we passed the point of no control. We were both breathing heavily. Kate opened her eyes, looking at me in confusion.

"What's the matter?"

"We need time before we jump back into a physical relationship," I said softly.

A range of emotions crossed her face as I continued, "How about we watch a movie now?"

"You want to watch a movie?"

There was a note of incredulity in her voice.

I grabbed her waist, set her back down on her feet, then rebuttoned my shirt. My panties were uncomfortably soaked.

"Make no mistake Kate, I want to fuck you so much that I'm shaking with it. But I promised we'd take it slow this time."

"But..."

I shook my head and grabbed her hand. "Come on, I haven't watched *Elf* yet this year. Let's watch it now. I know how much you love that one."

***

Last Christmas...

"You've never seen Elf? How is that possible?"

Kate shrugged. "I've never watched a lot of movies, and Christmas movies, well, they're so sappy."

I'd realized over the time we'd been together that Kate both loved and hated Christmas. It was like she liked the idea of Christmas but hadn't really experienced it the same way as other people.

"Not the funny ones, they're not sappy at all. Funny Christmas movies are the highlight of my year. Have you seen Scrooged?"

"No."

"Christmas Story? The Muppet Christmas Carol? National Lampoon's Christmas Vacation?"

"No, no, and no."

I pulled Kate toward me, wrapping my arms around her waist. "Oh grasshopper, I have so much to teach you about the true meaning of Christmas."

***

Kate and I settled on the couch, queuing up the movie and pulling a blanket over our laps. I'd turned down the lights, leaving the space lit only by the lights of the Christmas tree and the glow from the large screen TV on the wall.

It felt nice to have Kate in my house again, sitting on the couch next to me, even if she was a bit farther away than I preferred. I shifted, moving closer, then shifted again. I thought I was being subtle, but Kate laughed.

"What are you doing?"

"Getting closer to you," I admitted.

She shook her head slightly, then scooted over a few more inches until we were touching from shoulder to knee. I put my arm around her, and she snuggled into my side, resting the back of her head on my shoulder as the movie began.

We laughed together as Buddy had his big adventure in New York City, and by the time Santa's sleigh was fixed with the spirit of Christmas, we were laying down on the couch together, her back to my front, our legs tangled together.

As the credits rolled, Kate pushed herself up to a seated position.

"I should probably go," she said, reluctance clear in her voice.

When she got off the couch my body immediately mourned being close to her. I shivered from the sudden chill, then reminded myself that I was the one who'd insisted on putting the brakes on things.

Long game, Lucy, I reminded myself.

"Okay, I had fun tonight," I told her, reaching for her hand.

She smiled. "Me too. Thanks for dinner. And the movie."

"I'll walk you out." Slipping into my shoes and coat, I followed Kate to the street where she'd parked her ancient car.

"How's she running for you?" I asked, patting the hood.

I'd fixed Kate's car twice during the time we were dating, not including the radiator issue that had first brought us together. I knew she didn't make a lot of money at the hotel, but it really bothered me to see her driving around in a car that had so many issues.

"I had a battery issue recently, but other than that, it's been good." She avoided my eyes, making me wonder if there was more to the story, but I didn't push.

After pressing a quick kiss on my mouth, she slid into her car and quickly started it. The engine sounded rough, and I could tell she was burning oil. As soon as we were officially back together again, I was going to convince Kate to get a new car. I was fairly sure she could afford it, but even if she couldn't, I had several cars I was working on rebuilding at the moment. Maybe I could fix one up and give it to her for Christmas...

Kate

I turned over, punching my pillow, then sighed deeply. I could not get to sleep. Not after the evening I'd spent with Lucy. In some ways it had felt like we'd just fallen back into our previous relationship. Talking, cooking, watching movies. But there was still a tentativeness between us from the pain of our break-up.

Of course all that tentativeness had faded away once we got our hands on each other...

Maybe Lucy was right about taking things slow. I'd never gotten back together with an ex before, so I wasn't sure how it was supposed to feel. All I knew was that my mind and my heart were at odds. My heart wanted to accept Lucy's apology and pick up where we left off, while my mind tried to remind me to be smart. To protect myself.

And when she'd kissed me in the kitchen... I'd been feeling horny ever since, my empty pussy throbbing, begging to be filled. My fingers slid beneath the blankets of their own volition, and I closed my eyes, giving into the inevitable. I wasn't going to sleep until I could get some release. As my fingers slid inside my already slick folds, I pulled up my favorite memory.

*****

Last Christmas...

When I knocked on Lucy's door, she opened it almost immediately.

"Were you waiting at the door?" I asked, checking out her long shapely legs. Despite the fact that it was almost Christmas, she was wearing baggy shorts with an old Chicago Cubs tee shirt. And gym socks. Damn, she was adorable.

"I missed you terribly."

She made an exaggerated pouty face and I smiled.

"We just saw each other this morning," I reminded her.

We'd spent the night tangled in each other's arms, making each other come over and over again until we both fell into an exhausted sleep. Pretty much a typical night for us. Even after a few weeks together, we couldn't get enough of each other.

"This morning was too long ago," she pouted.

Lucy closed the door behind me, then shoved me against it, her mouth coming to mine like a heat-seeking missile. Grabbing my wrists, she pulled them up next to my head, pinning them against the door. She bit at my lower lip, demanding access to my mouth, and when I opened for her, she shoved her tongue inside, giving me a hot, claiming kiss that made my panties wet in about two seconds.

While we kissed, she rolled her hips against mine. I was a couple of inches taller than her, so with every roll she slid her pelvis upward, grinding over my clit with her own.

"Lucy." I gasped her name when she pulled away, lowering her head to kiss down my neck. She shoved the neckline of my shirt to the side with her nose, then caught the skin at the juncture of my shoulder between her sharp little teeth. She added suction, marking me like we were teenagers necking behind the bleachers after gym class. The pain was exquisite, heightening my arousal even more.

She released my hands, quickly shoving them under my shirt to roughly squeeze my breasts. I was making breathy little whining noises, already incredibly close to orgasm despite the fact that I was still wearing pants.

With my hands free now, I shoved her loose shorts down to her thighs, then came back for her panties. Lucy shimmied, making her shorts and underwear fall to her ankles even while she continued to suck on my neck.

When she pulled away, I could feel the mark throbbing. There was no doubt she'd given me a nice hickey.

"On the floor," she ordered, her voice deep and firm. She squeezed my boobs in emphasis.

I'd never seen Lucy like this before, never even had a hint of a dominant side in the short time we'd been together. But I liked it. I liked it a lot.

I lowered to my knees, thinking that she wanted me to lick her pussy, but she pressed a hand against my breastbone instead. "On your back."

I lowered to the floor, shrugging my coat off on the way, then kicked off my shoes. Lucy kneeled next to me, making quick work of removing the boring navy pants that I wore to work. Then she practically ripped off my plain cotton panties. No one had ever done that before, and I damn near came on the spot.

Lucy shoved between my legs, and I lifted them to wrap around her hips. Bracing herself with her elbows on the floor, she began sliding her pussy against mine roughly, pressing down as she rubbed against my clit.

I'd had women try this position before and get nowhere with it, but somehow Lucy was unerringly able to line us up just right and add just enough friction that it only took a few minutes before I felt the first signs of an impending orgasm.

"I'm close," I gasped. "Please Lucy."

I didn't really know what I was begging for, but clearly Lucy did because she ground down on my clit even harder while she lowered her head and bit my nipple right through my shirt and bra. Despite the barrier of fabric, when she caught the nipple between her teeth I came with a shriek. Bucking against her, I rolled my hips up to meet hers, eager to prolong the pleasure that was coursing through my body.

My vision cleared as I started to come down from my orgasm. I gasped for breath as Lucy continued to get herself off with my body, grinding hard against me. I knew she was close when her strokes started to falter.

Pulling her head down, I kissed her deeply as she started to shake with the force of her own pleasure. Rolling us over, I slid a finger inside her, fucking her with my finger while I rubbed the palm of my hand against her clit. Lucy rocked against my hand, practically sobbing with her force of her orgasm.

She was so beautiful when she came, her back arching up, her eyes screwed closed in ecstasy as she chanted my name like a prayer.

When she finally found her release, I cuddled next to her, resting my head on her shoulder while she caught her breath. Sensing her looking at me, I tilted my head up to meet her eyes.

"I fucking love you so much," she gasped.

I surged up to press a quick kiss against her lips.

"I love you too."

***

As the memory of that night with Lucy helped me bring myself to orgasm, I came to a decision. I had to give this relationship another chance. Sure, Lucy had hurt me – badly. But knowing a little more about her history and observing that she was impetuous and sometimes struggled to communicate, I believed her when she said she was sorry.

But if we were going to give this relationship another go, we needed to do a better job at communication. And I needed to find a way to forgive her for treating me like shit and triggering my biggest fear: abandonment.

Lucy

I grunted as I twisted the wrench, trying to loosen the rusted on bolt. A few days after Kate and I broke up I'd rescued this nineteen seventies MG Roadster from an impound lot where it likely had been languishing since before I was born. The mustard yellow sports car was my baby, and I'd spent the last six months lovingly restoring it while trying to recover from my broken heart.

It was probably going to take another six months – maybe more – before I was finished. This little car needed a lot of work to get back to her glory days.

Maybe it was weird that a mechanic restored cars to relax from a day job working on cars, but the truth was, almost every mechanic I knew tinkered with a passion project on the side.

The bolt finally gave way, and I disconnected the brake line from the master cylinder with a smile of triumph. I might not be the strongest person working on cars, but what I lacked in strength I made up for in tenacity.

The word tenacity made me think of Kate. Then again, everything made me think of Kate, if I was honest.

My mind flashed to the expression on her face when I pulled away from her last night when we were making out on the counter, insisting that we take things slow. I could have had sex with her, God knows I'd wanted nothing else, and I knew without a doubt that she'd felt the same. But we moved too fast the first time we'd been together, and without a base of trust, we'd folded like a house of cards.

Well, I'd folded. The truth was that Kate had always been completely up front with me, completely transparent. She'd shared her hopes and fears while I'd kept a lot of that to myself. I wasn't sure why exactly. Maybe just an innate sense of independence. Or maybe because I didn't want her to think I was a basket case.

Then I'd acted like a basket case anyway. And a mean one, at that. I'd been doing a lot of self-reflection lately and not liking what I saw, if I was perfectly honest. I needed to do some work on myself, and I needed to earn Kate's trust again. I planned to spend the rest of my life making it up to her. If she let me, that was.

As if thinking about her had conjured her, I heard a knock and then Kate stuck her head around the door of the garage at my parents' house. They had a giant double lot with a garage that was more like a barn, so my brother, father, and I all used it for our restoration projects.

"Hey there," I called out, warmth blooming inside me. I'd been having an internal struggle about calling her all day, but I didn't want to be too pushy.

"I hope it's okay that I dropped by," she said tentatively.

"You're always welcome here," I said firmly. "Come see my baby."

She entered the garage, walking around the Roadster with an admiring look.

"This car is so cool," she said enthusiastically. "You're going to keep this golden mustard color, right?"

"Oh yeah, but I have a lot more to do before she's ready to be repainted. When I found it in the junk yard she was in sad shape."

To the untrained eye, it probably looked to be in sad shape still, but I'd rebuilt a good portion of the engine so far. With a vehicle this old, there were always long delays for parts, which hampered my progress, but I was definitely making headway. I hoped that by this summer I could get her out on the road.

"Can we talk for a few minutes?" she asked.

Kate looked a little nervous, and my stomach lurched, wondering if she'd come here to tell me that she didn't want to see me anymore. I thought things had gone so well last night, but maybe she disagreed.

"Sure. I always have time for you."

I turned down the music I'd been playing while I worked, then headed to a mini fridge where we kept drinks and snacks.

"Water? Coke? Beer?"

"Water please," she said politely.

I grabbed two bottles of water, then led her to a little seating area we had set up in one corner. It wasn't unusual for me, my dad, or my brother to spend the day out here working on our passion projects, so when Mom remodeled the kitchen, Dad had moved the tables and chairs out here for us to use when we took a break.

"I know I should have called, but I wanted to talk in person," Kate began.

Nausea rose up, and I pressed my hand against my stomach protectively.

"It's fine," I bit out, trying not to puke.

I realized that my nerves were ridiculous given that I'd been the one to break up with her, but it had been a huge mistake. I'd known the minute I'd seen her at the mall, and it had just been reinforced during the time we'd spent together over the last week.

Now that we'd found each other again, I didn't want to let Kate go. I just hoped that she hadn't changed her mind about giving me another chance.

"I've been doing a lot of thinking, Lucy, and the thing is, I'm not sure if it's a good idea for me to date you again."

When I winced in pain, Kate leaned forward, taking my free hand and giving me the tiniest of smiles.

"Then again, I've never been one to have good ideas."

I froze, uncertain if I'd heard her correctly.

"Are you saying you'll forgive me?" I whispered.

"I already have. You were right before, I still am in love with you. And I've missed you, missed having you in my life."

My eyes widened so big I swear I could see my own brain.

"Um. Well. Then will you, uh, be my girlfriend again?" My heart was racing so fast I could scarcely get the words out.

Her smile widened.

"On one condition."

"Anything."

"I want to be the first person to ride in this adorable car when you get it fixed up."

"You got it."

We sat there staring at each other like loons for a full minute before I jumped to my feet, pulling her up next to me. I wrapped my arms around her shoulders, threading my fingers behind her neck, and stepped closer until just an inch separated our bodies.

"Don't make me sorry that I let you in again," she whispered, suddenly looking vulnerable.

"I promise you, I will never hurt you again. You're it for me, Kate. The one I want to spend the rest of my life with."

Her eyes widened, and I could tell she felt the same, but ever cautious, she neutralized her expression.

"Well, let's just see how things go for a while first before we make any big decisions, okay?"

I reached up to tuck a lock of hair behind her ear, then cupped her cheek in my hand, giving her a tender smile.

"You got it."

Kate

I closed the distance between our bodies, covering Lucy's mouth with my own. Now that I'd made the decision to forgive her, I felt lighter somehow. More at peace. The truth was, I knew instinctively that Lucy's behavior when she broke up with me was an aberration. Hell, I knew it at the time. We might not have spent that much time together in the grand scheme of things, but somehow, I still felt like I'd known her for my entire life.

We kissed until we were both breathless, our bodies pressed against each other. Lucy took my hand and walked towards her car, grabbing a blanket off a shelf as we went.

"Are we going to fool around in the back seat?" I asked.

"It doesn't have a back seat right now," she said. "Unfortunately, I found a family of mice living in the upholstery."

I came to a dead stop. "What?" I screeched, looking around like I thought the mice were going to attack me at any moment.

Lucy laughed. "Don't worry, I've resettled them all, far away from here. The car is now mouse free. But I didn't know you were afraid of mice."

"I hate all rodents," I said vehemently.

I didn't tell her that I'd spent a lifetime in crappy foster homes that often had rodents or bugs or both. But I could tell from the sympathetic look on her face that she'd guessed the truth.

"Well, my father wouldn't allow any non-human guests in his precious garage," she said lightly.

Lucy spread the blanket on the floor in front of the hood of the car she'd been working on. I knew from visiting here before that they kept a supply of old blankets to use when they needed to protect the paint on a car.

As I walked towards her, I realized that someone had put up a Christmas tree in the corner behind the car. The lights were on, casting multicolored shadows on the top of the car.

"You put up a Christmas tree in your garage?" I asked.

"Mom did. She said if we were going to spend some much time out here, we might as well have some Christmas cheer in the garage. You know how much my family loves Christmas."

Lucy pressed a button on her phone, and soft Christmas music played over the speakers. She lowered herself to the blanket, beckoning me to follow her. I looked around nervously.

"What about your family?"

"Mom and Dad are at my grandmother's fixing something, and my brother is at the garage. We'll be totally alone here." She lay down on her side, propping her head up with her hand. "We can be as naughty as we want."

"Okay then," I said, dropping to the blanket to join her. I'd already been humiliated in front of Lucy's family once, I didn't want to add to that by having them walk in on us naked and fooling around on the garage floor.

The minute I hit the blanket, Lucy was on me. She rolled me over and started kissing me like I was the oxygen she needed to breathe.

"Kate, oh my God, Kate," she said as she peppered little kisses down my jaw to my chin and then back up again. I wiggled beneath her, desperate for more.

"We're wearing too many clothes," I complained, tearing at the zipper of the mechanic overalls she was wearing.

"I'll race you!" she said, popping upright and practically ripping her clothes off.

As tempted as I was to enjoy the show, I was dying to relieve the ache between my legs too. I pulled my sweater over my head, unfastened my bra, and wiggled out of my leggings and panties in record time. When we were both completely naked, we rolled towards each other again, a tangle of limbs as we kissed and teased and stroked each other's bodies until we were both shaking with need.

"How about you sit on my face?" Lucy suggested.

She'd told me once that she loved the feeling of being smothered by my pussy, and I loved it too, but for our first time together after such a long absence, I wanted something more intimate. I shook my head.

"Maybe later. Right now, I want us to come together."

Lucy immediately turned around, stretching out next to me, matching her bottom with my top in one of our favorite positions. Almost perfectly in sync, we lowered our heads and went for each other's pussies. I sighed deeply as I got my first taste of Lucy's cream on my tongue. I licked up and down her channel as she did the same to me.

I struggled to focus as she started tapping the tip of her tongue against my already swollen clit. Desperate to get her off so I could come, I slid my finger into her opening, then quickly added a second, stroking around her walls until I found the rough patch of her G spot. Lucy made a keening noise against my vag, something between a howl and a whine.

When I stroked her some more while licking over her clit, Lucy copied my movements, inserting her own finger into my channel. She sucked my clit into her mouth, biting down lightly, and I didn't need a second finger before I was flying towards my orgasm.

"Lucy!"

My entire body stiffened as my orgasm crashed through my body like a tsunami hitting the shore. I saw black spots in my vision, and I could hear my heart pounding in my ears as I trembled beside Lucy.

Somehow, I was able to keep fucking Lucy with my fingers, and she ground herself against me with increasing urgency. It only took another few seconds before she groaned my name and came all over my hand, soaking my fingers.

Slowly, I pulled away and flopped over onto my back, gasping for breath as a sense of euphoria filled my mind.

Lucy recovered first, shifting on top of me, our bodies pressed together as our mouths found each other again. My hips rocked up against hers, still shaking with aftershocks. I couldn't get enough of this woman.

"Just give me a few minutes," Lucy whispered. "I want to make you come again after I can feel my fingers again."

"Maybe I want to make you come again instead," I said sassily.

She leaned down and gently bit my earlobe. "Don't worry, we've got the rest of our lives to make love."

And then she fell asleep in my arms, right there in the middle of the garage.

Epilogue – Lucy

Valentine's Day...

"Are you sure about this, sis? You two have only been back together for what? Two months?"

"Two months plus the six months we dated originally." I answered. "But since we've been back together again, everything has been perfect."

I studied the ring in my hand with a smile. Kate was going to love it, I just knew it.

Denise frowned. "Not to be a Debbie Downer, but you thought everything was perfect last time. What's different now?"

"Um, promise not to tell anyone this?"

If my other siblings got wind of what I was doing, I would never hear the end of it.

My sister's gaze snapped from the engagement ring in my hand to my face.

"I promise, what's the big secret?"

"I've been seeing a counselor."

"A counselor? You mean like a therapist counselor?"

I nodded. "Yeah, when I got back together with Kate, I realized that I needed to do some work on myself to be a good partner for her. I rushed things the first time, then freaked out and dumped her the first time I thought something was going wrong."

"In fairness, you thought she was cheating on you," my loyal sister reminded me.

"Yeah, but I assumed that was what was going on because it had happened to me before, with that girl I dated in college, Sonia. I let my past trauma cloud my vision of the present."

"Did your therapist tell you that?" Denise asked skeptically.

"Yeah. She's been super helpful."

"How come you're the one who needs to be fixed in this relationship?"

I loved how protective my sister was, but this time it was misplaced.

"No. Funnily enough, when I told Kate I was going to counseling, she shared that she had started going herself right after we ran into each other at the mall. We've both been working on ourselves and working together on communication and trust."

My sister was silent for a long moment before her face softened. "Are you happy, Lucy?"

"I am. I love Kate and I want to spend the rest of my life with her."

"Well, that's all I want for you then. Besides, I love Kate too, the whole family does. I just don't want to have to watch you go through another devastating break-up."

Denise shuddered dramatically, as if it had been as hard for her to watch as it was for me and Kate to go through it.

"No break-up this time," I promised. "But I'm hoping for an engagement tonight."

We both startled when we heard a knock on the door.

"Okay, get the hell out of here so I can propose to my girlfriend on Valentine's Day," I said, giving her a gentle shove.

Denise pulled me into her arms, giving me a tight hug before heading for the front door with me right on her heels. My sister opened the door, and there was the love of my life. Kate was wearing a trench coat that she'd opened wide, holding it open to reveal that she was only wearing red heart pasties on her tits and a teeny tiny pair of red panties.

Kate squeaked when she realized it was Denise at the door, her face immediately turning as red as her pasties. My sister clamped her hand over her eyes and groaned.

"It's for you," she called over her shoulder as she blindly shuffled past Kate and practically ran down the stairs towards her car.

Kate stood on the porch frozen in shock.

"Hey, if you don't want to share that view with someone else, you might want to come in."

"Shit." She clutched the edges of the trench coat together, looking completely mortified.

I grabbed her by the coat, shoving it off her shoulders the second she was safely inside the house. I damn near swallowed my tongue as I got a better view of her outfit, such as it was.

"Happy Valentine's Day!" Kate said cheerfully, apparently recovered from her embarrassment.

"That is the sexiest damned thing I've seen in my life," I said, my voice sounding hoarse as I studied her beautiful body.

"You haven't seen the best part," she smirked, turning around to reveal the generous curve of her ass, totally bare other than the fabric heart that connected the waistband with the G-string. A flood of moisture soaked my panties.

"Sweet merciful Jesus," I whispered. "My Valentine's dreams are coming true."

Kate turned back around. "Well, you've made my dreams come true, so it's only fair."

"Not yet," I said.

"Not yet, what?" she asked in confusion.

"I haven't made all of our dreams come true yet, but I'm hoping this will get us closer."

I dropped to one knee, holding out the ring I'd slipped into my pocket when she knocked on the door.

"Kate, will you do me the honor of becoming my wife?"

She stared at the ring in my palm, her eyes filling with tears. I held my breath, hoping that Denise wasn't right that it was too soon.

Kate dropped to her knees, taking the ring out of my hand and looking at it almost reverently. It was a simple ring, gold with three small inset diamonds. I knew that my girlfriend didn't like excessively fancy stuff. Besides, we both worked with our hands, so it was important to have jewelry that wouldn't get caught on something.

"Well? Are you going to keep me in suspense?" I nudged.

Kate looked from the ring to my face, then she gave me a huge smile. "Yes! Yes, I will marry you, Lucy. Oh my God!"

I slid the ring on her finger and pulled her into my arms, kissing her until we were both breathless.

"How about we get married next Christmas?" I suggested. "Since Christmas is our anniversary twice over."

"I love it," she said immediately. "I love you so much, Lucy."

"I love you too. I can't wait to spend the rest of our lives together."

***

The Christmas before last...

"If you ladies are ready, we're about to close for the night."

I looked around the restaurant in surprise, not noticing how it had emptied out. After dropping off her car at the garage for my father to work on, Kate and I spent hours talking at the little diner up the street. After talking and laughing for hours, I was completely smitten with her in a way that I'd never experienced before.

I handed the long-suffering waitress my credit card to settle the bill, then leaned forward on the table, staring into Kate's eyes like I could look into her soul.

"Do you believe in fate?" I asked.

"Not really," she said. "Why?"

"Because I think fate brought us together today."

"I thought it was a bad radiator hose," she teased. I loved that we'd known each other less than a day and we were already bantering like we'd known each other forever.

"Whether it was fate or your radiator, there's one thing I know for sure, Kate."

"What?"

"I'm going to spend the rest of my life with you."

***

You can find more of Reba's lesbian romances at
Books2read.com/rl/lesbianromance[1]

If you liked this book, please consider leaving a review or rating to let me know. Keep reading for a preview of Reba Bale's lesbian romance book, "The Divorcee's First Time".

Be sure to join my newsletter for more great books. You'll receive a free book when you join my newsletter. Subscribers are the first to hear about all of my new releases and sales. Visit my mailing list sign-up at bit.ly/ RebaBaleSapphic[2] to download your free book today.

---

1. *https://books2read.com/rl/lesbianromance*

2. https://bit.ly/RebaBaleSapphic

Special Preview

The Divorcee's First Time
A Contemporary Lesbian Romance
By Reba Bale

"It's done," I said triumphantly. "My divorce is final."

My best friend Susan paused in the process of sliding into the restaurant booth, her sharply manicured eyebrows raising almost to her hairline. "Dickhead finally signed the papers?" she asked, her tone hopeful.

I nodded as Susan settled into the seat across from me. "The judge signed off on it today. Apparently his barely legal girlfriend is knocked up, and she wants to get a ring on her finger before the big event." I explained with a touch of irony in my voice. "The child bride finally got it done for me."

Susan smiled and nodded. "Well congratulations and good riddance. Let's order some wine."

We were most of the way through our second bottle when the conversation turned back to my ex. "I wonder if Dickhead and his Child Bride will last for the long haul," Susan mused.

I shook my head and blew a chunk of hair away from my mouth.

"I doubt it," I told her. "Someday she's gonna roll over and think, there's got to be something better out there than a self-absorbed man child who doesn't know a clitoris from a doorknob."

Susan laughed, sputtering her wine. I eyed her across the table. Although she was ten years older than me, we had been best friends for the last five years. We worked together at the accounting firm. She had been my trainer when I first came there, fresh out of school with my degree. We bonded over work, but soon realized that we were kindred spirits.

Susan was rapidly approaching forty but could easily pass for my age. Her hair was black and shiny, hinting at her Puerto Rican heritage, with blunt bangs and blond highlights that she paid a fortune for. Her face was clear and unlined, with large brown eyes and cheek bones that could cut glass. She was an avid runner and worked hard to maintain a slim physique since the women in her family ran towards the chunkier side.

I was almost her complete opposite. Blonde curls to her straight dark hair, blue eyes instead of brown, curvy where she was lean, introverted to her extrovert.

But somehow, we clicked. We were closer than sisters. Honestly, I don't know how I would have gotten through the last year without her. She had been the first one I called when my marriage fell apart, and she had supported me throughout the whole process.

It had been a big shock when I came home early one day and found my husband getting a blow job in the middle of our living room. It had been even more shocking when I saw the fresh young face at the other end of that blow job.

"What the fuck are you doing?" I had screeched, startling them both out of their sex stupor. "You're getting blow jobs from children now?"

The girl had looked up from her knees with eyes glowing in righteous indignation. "I'm not a child, I'm nineteen," she had informed me proudly. "I'm glad you finally found out. I give him what you don't, and he loves me."

I looked into the familiar eyes of my husband and saw the panic and confusion there. I made it easy for him. "Get out," I told him firmly, my voice leaving no room for argument. "Take your teenage girlfriend and get the fuck out. We're getting a divorce. Expect to hear from my lawyer."

The condo was in my name. I had purchased it before we were married, and since I had never added his name to the deed, he had no rights to it. There was no question he would be the one leaving.

My husband just stared at me with his jaw hanging open like he couldn't believe it. "But Jennifer," he whined. "You don't understand. Let me explain."

"There's nothing to understand," I told him sadly. "This is a deal breaker for me, and you know that as well as I do. We are done."

The girl had taken his hand and smiled triumphantly. "Come on baby," she told him. "Zip up and let's get out of here. We can finally be together like we planned."

"Yeah baby," I had sneered. "I'll box up your stuff. It'll be in the hallway tomorrow. Pick it up by six o'clock or I'm trashing it all."

After they left my first call was to the locksmith, but my second call was to Susan.

That night was the last time I had seen my husband until we had met for the court-ordered pre-divorce mediation. He spent most of that session reiterating what he had told me in numerous voice mails, emails and sessions spent yelling on the other side of my front door. He loved me. He had made a terrible mistake. He wasn't going to sign the papers. We were meant to be together. Needless to say, mediation hadn't been very successful. Fortunately, I had been careful to keep our assets separate, as if I knew that someday I would be in this situation.

Through it all, Susan had been my rock. In the end I don't think I was even that sad about the divorce, I was really angrier with myself for staying in a relationship that wasn't fulfilling with a man I didn't love anymore.

"You need to get some quality sex." Susan drew my attention back to the present. "Bang him out of your system."

"I don't know," I answered slowly. "I think I need a hiatus."

"A hiatus from what?" Susan asked with a frown. "You haven't had sex in what, eighteen months?"

I nodded. "Yeah, but I just can't take a disappointing fumble right now. I would rather have nothing than another three-pump chump."

I shook my head and continued, "I'm going to stick with my battery-operated boyfriend, he never disappoints me."

Susan smiled. "That's because you know your way around your own vajayjay."

She motioned to the waiter to bring us a third bottle of wine.

"That's why I like to date women," she continued. "We already know our way around the equipment."

I nodded thoughtfully. "You make a good point."

Susan leaned forward. "We've never talked about this," she said earnestly. "Have you ever been with a woman?"

For more of the story, check out "The Divorcee's First Time" by Reba Bale, available for immediate download[1] today.

***

Want a free book? Join my newsletter and a special gift. I'll contact you a few times a month with story updates, new releases, and special sales. Visit bit.ly/RebaBaleSapphic[2] for more information.

---

1.   https://books2read.com/u/bpznKX

2. https://bit.ly/RebaBaleSapphic

Other Books by Reba Bale

Check out my other books, available on most major online retailers now. Go to my webpage[1] at bit.ly/AuthorRebaBale to learn more.

Friends to Lovers Lesbian Romance Series
The Divorcee's First Time
My BFF's Sister
My Rockstar Assistant
My College Crush
My Fake Girlfriend
My Secret Crush
My Holiday Love
My Valentine's Gift
My Spring Fling
My Forbidden Love
My Office Wife
My Second Chance
Coming Out in Ten Dates
Worth Waiting For
The Surrender Club Lesbian Romance Series
Jaded
Hated
Fated
Saved
Caged
The Sapphic Security Series
Guarding the Senator's Daughter

---

1. https://books2read.com/ap/nB2qJv/Reba-Bale

Menage Romances

Pie Promises
Tornado Warning
Summer in Paradise
Life of the Mardi
Bases Loaded
Two for One Deal

The Unexpectedly Mine Series

Sinful Desires
Taken by Surprise
Just One Night
Forbidden Desires

Hotwife Erotic Romances

Hotwife in the Woods
Hotwife on the Beach
Hotwife Under the Tree
A Hotwife's Retreat
Hot Wife Happy Life

Want a free book? Just join my newsletter at bit.ly/RebaBaleSapphic[2]*.*
You'll be the first to hear about new releases, special sales, and free
offers.

About the Author

Reba Bale writes erotic romance, lesbian romance, menage romance, & the spicy stories you want to read on a cold winter's night. When Reba is not writing she is reading the same naughty stories she likes to write.

You can also follow Reba on Ream at reamstories.com/rebabale[3] for free stories, bonus epilogues and more. You can also hear all about new releases and special sales by joining Reba's newsletter mailing list.[4]

---

3.   https://reamstories.com/rebabale

4.   https://bit.ly/rebabooks

Don't miss out!

Visit the website below and you can sign up to receive emails whenever Reba Bale publishes a new book. There's no charge and no obligation.

https://books2read.com/r/B-A-IDTM-YOURC

BOOKS 2 READ

Connecting independent readers to independent writers.